A NOTE TO PARENTS

When your children are ready to "step into reading," giving them the right books—and lots of them—is as crucial as giving them the right food to eat. **Step into Reading Books** present exciting stories and information reinforced with lively, colorful illustrations that make learning to read fun, satisfying, and worthwhile. They are priced so that acquiring an entire library of them is affordable. And they are beginning readers with an important difference—they're written on four levels.

Step 1 Books, with their very large type and extremely simple vocabulary, have been created for the very youngest readers. **Step 2 Books** are both longer and slightly more difficult. **Step 3 Books,** written to mid-second-grade reading levels, are for the child who has acquired even greater reading skills. **Step 4 Books** offer exciting nonfiction for the increasingly proficient reader.

Children develop at different ages. **Step into Reading Books,** with their four levels of reading, are designed to help children become good—and interested—readers *faster*. The grade levels assigned to the four steps—preschool through grade 1 for Step 1, grades 1 through 3 for Step 2, grades 2 and 3 for Step 3, and grades 2 through 4 for Step 4—are intended only as guides. Some children move through all four steps very rapidly; others climb the steps over a period of several years. These books will help your child "step into reading" in style!

Library of Congress Cataloging-in-Publication Data
Hautzig, Deborah.
    Aladdin and the magic lamp / retold by Deborah Hautzig ; illustrated by Kathy Mitchell.
        p.   cm. – (Step into reading. A Step 3 book)
    Summary: With the aid of a genie from a magic lamp, Aladdin fights an evil magician and
wins the hand of a beautiful princess.
    ISBN 0-679-83241-6 (pbk.) – ISBN 0-679-93241-0 (lib. bdg.)
    [1. Fairy tales. 2. Folklore, Arab.]   I. Mitchell, Kathy, ill.   II. Aladdin.   III. Title.
    IV. Series: Step into reading. Step 3 book. PZ8.H2944A1 1993   398.21–dc20   [E]   92-1608

Manufactured in the United States of America 10 9 8 7 6 5

STEP INTO READING is a trademark of Random House, Inc.

Step into Reading

Aladdin
AND THE
MAGIC LAMP

retold by Deborah Hautzig
illustrated by Kathy Mitchell

A Step 3 Book

Random House 🏠 New York

Once upon a time, in Persia,
there lived a poor widow
and her son, Aladdin.
Aladdin's father had been a tailor.

When he died, he left no money for his family. So Aladdin's mother had to work day and night to support herself and her son.

One morning a strange man came to
town and saw Aladdin playing in the
street. The man was a powerful magician
from Egypt. He watched Aladdin closely.

The magician saw that Aladdin was

small and poor and innocent. He had use
for just such a boy.

"This is the boy I've been looking
for," he said. "And I know just how to
win his trust!"

Secretly, the magician asked the other children about the boy. Then he spoke to Aladdin himself.

"Are you Aladdin, the tailor's son?"
he asked.

Aladdin was surprised that the man
knew his name.

"Yes," he replied, "but my father
is dead."

The magician threw his arms around
Aladdin. "I am your uncle, your father's
long-lost brother!"

The magician was lying, of course. He
was not Aladdin's uncle at all!

Then the magician gave Aladdin some
pieces of gold and said: "Give these to
your mother. Tell her your uncle is here
and will come to visit."

Aladdin gladly took the gold home.

"Mother, my uncle is coming to visit!"
cried Aladdin.

Aladdin's mother frowned. "Your
uncle?" she said. "It can't be! Your uncle
disappeared years ago!"

"But he *must* be my uncle. Look at
what he gave us!"

Aladdin showed his mother the shiny
gold coins. She gasped.

"You are right, my son," she said. "He
must be your uncle. I must prepare a fine
meal for him! How I wish your father
were here!"

The magician arrived with gifts of
fruit and wine. He had a fine meal with
Aladdin and his mother.

"You have been very kind to us,"
said Aladdin's mother. "How can we
repay you?"

The magician smiled and said, "By
letting me take Aladdin for a walk. That
would make me very happy indeed."

"Go, with my blessing!" she said.

Aladdin and the magician went for a
walk outside the city gates. They walked

for a long time until at last they came
to a hilltop.

"Why are we here, Uncle?" asked
Aladdin.

"To see something wonderful," said
the magician. "First, you must gather
sticks to build a fire."

Aladdin did as he was told.

Soon a fire was blazing. The magician
stood over it and threw some sparkling
powder onto the flames.

"Abracadabra malla goo poof!" said the
magician. Instantly, the earth opened up!
And there lay a flat stone with a brass
ring in the middle.

Aladdin was terrified. He tried to run away, but the magician grabbed him and said: "Obey me! Beneath this stone lies a treasure, which will be ours. But you must do exactly as I say!"

The magician told him to pull the brass ring. Aladdin obeyed. The stone came up easily.

A small hole led down into a deep, dark cave. The magician was too big to fit through the hole, but Aladdin was just the right size.

"Go down," said the magician. "You will find a garden of fine fruit. In the garden you will find a lighted lamp. Bring it to me."

The magician took a ring from his finger and gave it to Aladdin. "This ring will protect you. Now go!"

Aladdin went down into the cave, and

came to the garden. Dazzling fruits of
every color hung from the trees. Aladdin
did not know that the fruits were really
jewels—diamonds and pearls, emeralds
and rubies! But he thought his mother
might like them. So he picked as many as
he could and filled his pockets. Then he
tied the lamp around his waist.

"Uncle," called Aladdin, "give me your hand and help me out!"

"First give me the lamp," said the magician.

"I can't!" said Aladdin.

"Give me the lamp!" the magician shouted.

"I can't. I need both hands," said Aladdin.

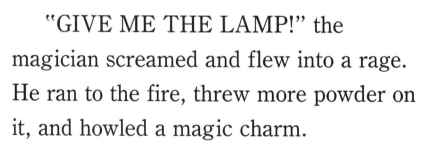

"GIVE ME THE LAMP!" the magician screamed and flew into a rage. He ran to the fire, threw more powder on it, and howled a magic charm.

At once, the stone moved back into its place. The earth closed, and Aladdin was trapped underground!

For two days, poor Aladdin sat below the earth and cried. He beat at the stone with his fists until his hands bled, but it would not move. He shouted and shouted for help, but no one heard him. At last, he clasped his hands to pray for help. When he did this, he touched the ring on his

finger, which the magician had left without taking. An enormous genie rose before him!

"I am the slave of the ring," said the genie. "What is your wish?"

Aladdin said, "Please! Get me out of here!"

The earth opened at once and Aladdin found himself outside.

Aladdin ran home and gave his mother the fruits. Then he told her all that had happened.

"But at least I have the lamp. I can sell it for food."

The lamp was very dirty, so Aladdin's mother began to rub it clean. *Poof!* Instantly, a huge genie appeared.

"I am the genie of the lamp," he boomed. "What is your wish?"

Aladdin's mother was terrified. But Aladdin said, "Get us something to eat."

The genie produced twelve silver plates piled high with delicious food. Aladdin and his mother were delighted.

"This lamp will change our lives," said Aladdin.

Aladdin and his mother lived happily for many years, thanks to the magic lamp. They had plenty of food and fine clothing.

One day Aladdin heard an order from the Sultan: "Everyone must stay home and close the shutters while my daughter, the Princess, goes to the bathhouse."

Aladdin was so curious to see her face! But this was very hard to do, because the Princess always wore a veil.

Aladdin hid behind the door of the bathhouse and peeped through a crack.

As the Princess went in, she lifted her veil. Aladdin gasped. She was so beautiful! Aladdin fell in love with her right away.

Aladdin slowly walked home. All he
could think about was the Princess.

"Mother," he cried, "I am in love with
the Princess. I have to marry her!"

"Don't talk nonsense," said his
mother. "The Sultan will never let you
do that!"

But Aladdin would not give up. He
begged his mother to go and speak to the
Sultan. At last she agreed. She took the

dazzling fruits that Aladdin had found in
the cave.

Trembling, Aladdin's mother kneeled before the Sultan.

"Your Highness, my son, Aladdin, is deeply in love with the Princess," she said. "He wishes to marry her."

Aladdin's mother held out the fruits.

The Sultan stared at the jewels. "Your son must love the Princess very much to send such gifts. But I have to be sure his love is true. Tell him to send forty gold

basins filled with jewels. They must be carried by eighty servants dressed as kings."

Aladdin's mother bowed to the Sultan and went home to give Aladdin the news.

When Aladdin heard the Sultan's
request, he rubbed his magic lamp.

"What is your wish?" thundered the
genie.

"I wish to have eighty servants
dressed as kings. I want them to carry
forty gold basins of jewels to the royal
palace," Aladdin commanded.

Instantly, his wish came true. The servants lifted the basins and marched toward the palace. Aladdin and his mother were close behind.

The Sultan could hardly believe his eyes. "Aladdin," he declared, "you have proved yourself worthy of the Princess. Marry her with my blessing."

Aladdin was overjoyed!

He called the genie and said: "Build me a palace made of the finest marble. Decorate the walls with emeralds and rubies and diamonds. There must be stables, and horses, and servants for my dear mother and for the Princess and me."

The very next day the palace was there! The genie had even laid a velvet carpet from Aladdin's palace to the Sultan's.

Aladdin rode an elegant horse to the Sultan's palace. Trumpets blared and cymbals crashed.

The wedding was grand! There was a huge feast, and the Princess and Aladdin danced until midnight.

Aladdin won the hearts of the people with his kind ways. He never forgot what it was like to be poor. He was polite and modest, and he always helped anyone in need. He and the Princess lived happily for several years.

But far away in Egypt, the magician found out that Aladdin had escaped from the cave. He knew that the rich and wonderful life Aladdin was living was all because of the magic lamp. The magician was furious! He vowed to get the lamp— and to destroy Aladdin.

The magician traveled night and day until he came to Persia. He bought some shiny copper lamps. Dressed as a beggar, he went to Aladdin's palace.

Aladdin was out hunting when the Princess saw a beggar outside her window.

"New lamps for old!" cried the beggar. "Give me your old lamps. I will give you new ones!"

The Princess gave him Aladdin's
dusty lamp. She did not know it was
magic.

"Give me a new lamp for this,"
she said.

"Gladly, Your Highness," said the
magician. He gave her a new lamp. Then
he grabbed Aladdin's lamp and ran.

The magician rubbed the lamp, and the genie appeared.

"Take Aladdin's palace, with me and the Princess in it, far away to Egypt!"

The genie did as he was told.

The Sultan looked toward Aladdin's palace and rubbed his eyes. It was GONE!

When Aladdin came home from hunting, only the Sultan was there to greet him. He grabbed Aladdin and shouted: "Where is the palace? And WHERE IS MY DAUGHTER?"

Aladdin was so shocked, he could not speak.

"Find the Princess—OR I WILL CUT OFF YOUR HEAD!" screamed the Sultan.

Aladdin was frantic. He searched
for many miles. But finally, he could not
go on. He sat down and clasped his hands
to pray.

The slave of the ring appeared!
Aladdin had forgotten he still wore the
magic ring.

"Save my life," begged Aladdin.
"Bring my palace and my Princess back!"

"I am not powerful enough. Only the genie of the lamp can do that," said the slave.

"Then take me to the palace."

Whoosh! The next moment, Aladdin was in Egypt, right outside his palace! The Princess was looking out her window. When she saw Aladdin, she cried for joy.

Aladdin kissed her and said, "I beg of you, tell me what has happened to my old lamp?"

The Princess told Aladdin.

"Now I know!" cried Aladdin. "It's the evil magician who did this. Where is the lamp?"

"He carries it with him. He wants me to marry him. He told me you were dead!"

Aladdin had to get the lamp back. But how? He had an idea. He went to the city to buy some poison powder. Then he returned to the palace.

"Listen carefully," Aladdin told the
Princess. "Ask the magician to have
supper with you. Then tell him you want
to taste the wine from his cellar. When
he goes to get it, put this powder in
your cup."

"In *my* cup?" said the Princess.

"Yes," said Aladdin. Then he
whispered in her ear.

The Princess put on her prettiest
dress. Then she asked the magician to
have supper with her. "I want to taste the
wine from your cellar," she said.

The magician hurried to his cellar
to get the wine. The instant he left,
the Princess put the poison powder
in her cup.

The magician returned and poured
the wine.

Then the Princess said, "It is good
luck to drink from your lover's cup. Will
you drink to my health?"

"Gladly," said the magician. He took

her cup, lifted it to his lips, and drank.
A second later, he grabbed his throat and
dropped to the floor.

He was dead!

The Princess and Aladdin fell into
each other's arms.

Then Aladdin took the lamp from the
magician's robe. He rubbed it, and the
genie appeared.

"Genie," said Aladdin, "take this
palace and everything in it back to
Persia!"

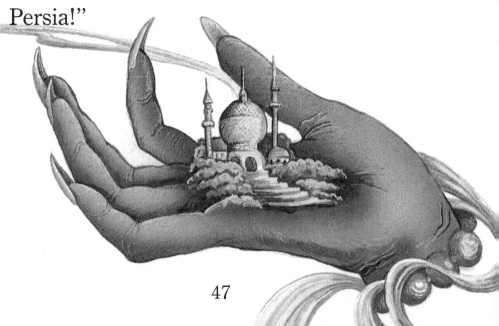

In Persia, the Sultan looked up and rubbed his eyes. There was Aladdin's palace! He shouted for joy.

Aladdin and the Princess told the Sultan about all that had happened. The Sultan ordered a ten-day feast.

"Everyone in the kingdom will celebrate the safe return of Aladdin and the Princess!" he said. "May they live happily ever after!"

And that is just what they did.